Left On Ice

IVY GLEN
BOOK 0.5

NOELLE STONE

*For everyone who knows that the real thrill is when the gloves
come off*

GLIDING ACROSS THE ICE, MY HEART POUNDS IN MY ears as I approach the goal. Two seconds left, I take my shot, and the blare of the buzzer rings in my ears as the puck hits the back of the net. My teammates rush together in celebration of our close-call victory, but I'm already skating off the ice, ripping my helmet off as I approach Abbie, who is waiting for me outside the rink.

"Girl, that is some serious helmet hair." Abbie's freckled nose wrinkles at me as I run past her, her shoulder-length brown hair swaying as I shove my helmet into her arms. Without slowing down, I turn slightly, giving her a good view of my middle finger. She laughs and follows me as I rush to the locker room that's situated between the two ice rinks of the rec center.

It's just my luck that mine and Carter's championship games would be scheduled at almost the same time. I guess this is what I get for continuing to want to play on the all-female team at our town's rec center instead of the high school team. I'll only catch the last 10 minutes of the game if I'm lucky. I pull my skates and pads off, throwing on my shoes from my locker. I turn just in time to see Abbie hoist my bag on top of my locker, ready for me to grab later.

I'm lucky to have a friend like her, someone who does whatever it takes to help me not tragically miss the most important game of my boyfriend's life, even if that means managing my heavy-ass duffel bag.

Ripping the hair tie out of my ponytail, I quickly run my fingers through my auburn hair, braiding it back.

Luckily, the locker rooms are right in the middle of the two ice rinks, so all we have to do is go through the door on the opposite side of the locker room to get to Carter's game.

The sound of the loud crowd greets me as I push the doors open, Abbie and I making our way to the front of the stands. I quickly scan the ice, trying to find Carter. Our schools' team, the Wolverines, are playing their long-standing rivals, the Sharks. The game is in a time-out, and I spot Carter in the huddle by the number on his jersey - 10, which gives me time to find our seats without missing any gameplay. The scoreboard shows a tie, 3-3, with five minutes left in the game.

Gwen said she would save us seats, so I focus on finding the head of wild blonde curls that act as a beacon. A couple of juniors on the JV hockey team wave to me as we move along the aisle, and I absentmindedly wave back, looking for Gwen. Her mane sticks out in the crowd, and we make a beeline towards her and the two empty spots she was saving for us.

"Gwen!" Despite the chatter of the crowd, she hears me, and her gaze flies to us as we sidle past some sophomores to get to her. "You're a lifesaver, Gwen. Thanks for the seats."

Spotting Carter's parents a couple of rows up, I wave at them. Mrs. Williams smiles warmly while Mr. Williams is so focused on the game, he doesn't even notice me.

As we settle, Gwen smiles widely at us, but a scowl quickly crosses her adorable face as she looks at something behind me, making her look like an angry kitten. Pulling me close, she attempts to shout-whisper into my ear, "Careful of those bitch-es," as her hazel eyes dart towards the sophomores further down the bench. "I heard them talking about how sexy Carter is and how they could 'fulfill his needs' better than you can."

A laugh bursts out of me, causing Gwen to furrow her brows and Abbie to roll her eyes. This isn't the first time some lower classmen have made ridiculous comments about my boyfriend, and it certainly won't be the last.

"Thanks for looking out for me, Gwennie." I press a quick kiss to her cheek. "But, Carter's been *mine* for the last three years," I make my voice loud enough for the sophomores next to us to hear. "It'll take more than some second rank skanks to drag him away from me."

Their sounds of indignation are like music to my ears and both Abbie and Gwen giggle as the aforementioned skanks scoot further down the bench from us, crossing their arms in anger.

Good. They should know that Carter wouldn't give them the time of day.

In Ivy Glen, a small town where ice hockey reigns supreme, Carter is the town's golden boy. It's only natural that everyone else wants a piece of him, no matter how many times he's made it abundantly clear that I'm the only girl for him.

Popular, charismatic, and gorgeous, he's friends with every-one. Even, unfortunately, girls who think they can swipe him out from under me. My heart warms at the fact that I know he only has eyes for me.

We've been inseparable since first grade. He claims he fell in love with the moment he saw me. But every time I bring up that it took him until the end of our freshman year of highschool to ask me out, he says that his "immature boy brain" didn't realize his feelings until then.

In my opinion, when we both started playing ice hockey in middle school at the Ivy Glen Rec Center, it bridged the gap that had been caused by emerging hormones and awkward phases. Allowing us to grow closer when other boys and girls would have grown apart.

The sound of a whistle blowing as the referee calls the end of the timeout has me snapping my attention back to the ice, waiting with bated breath as I see Carter getting ready to hop back into the rink. The assistant coach, who also happens to be my brother, Tom, must have spotted me because he claps him on the shoulder and says something close to his ear. Carter's gaze immediately finds me, his black hair peeking out from under his helmet, and an unrestrained grin breaks out on his face when he sees me, and mouths, *"You win?"*

Biting my lip, I nod my head once, and he winks at me before launching himself into the rink, causing my stomach to flip. Turning his attention to the game, he lines up for the face-off.

The Wolverines get possession of the puck and everyone's moving towards the goal. He glides along the ice like a fucking predator, beautiful and deadly. What does it say about me that my thighs clench together when he checks the other team's defenseman into the boards?

The whistle blows again, causing the surrounding crowd to groan in frustration. The ref is calling offsides, and at the faceoff, the other team gets possession of the puck.

Two minutes left. Shit.

The Shark's left winger has the puck and is gunning it for our net. A Wolverines defenseman rushes him, forcing the winger to pass the puck to their center forward. The crowd explodes as Carter swoops in, intercepting the pass.

We're all on our feet screaming as Carter rushes for the goal.

One minute.

Crying out with the rest of the crowd as Carter weaves in and out of the other team's players, sending the puck to one of his teammates, Jake. An almost imperceptible nod passes between the two of them as Carter skates to the right side of the goal while Jake approaches the goal from the left with the puck.

Jake fakes the shot, causing the goalie to shuffle, but instead, passes it to Carter. Before the goalie can correct his mistake, Carter takes his shot, and the puck hits the back of the net.

The buzzer beeps just as the scoreboard changes, leaving the score, 4-3, Ivy Glen Wolverines winning the championship. The cheers are almost deafening, but it's nothing compared to the way my heart pounds in my ears at the sight of Carter ripping his helmet off, his black hair flopping into his piercing blue eyes as his teammates rush the ice, crowding him and lifting their hockey sticks in celebration.

His eyes light up, laughing at his team's antics before Carter's gaze finds mine, and the weight of his stare has me licking my lips. His eyes dart down to my mouth, and fire pools low in my belly.

Fuck it. Tonight's the night.

I had planned on waiting to lose my virginity until after graduation. There was this idea in my head that I would somehow be more responsible if I waited until I was out of high-school, but this can't wait any longer. Tonight, I'll make Carter mine in every conceivable way.

Carter keeps my gaze as he shoves his way through his teammates, skating off the ice to the player bench area. They bristle at being pushed away at first, but get huge grins when they see that he's looking at me. Standing, I rush down the aisle towards the rink. We meet in the middle, him exiting the players' bench area and staring at me like he wants to devour me. I throw my arms around his neck as he captures my lips in a searing kiss. Whistles and whooping break out behind us as his arms snakes around my back, his tongue finding its way into my mouth. He's lifting me with one arm as he kisses me, and I don't care that we have an audience. A little moan escapes me as he crushes me to his chest.

I'd let him take me right here and now if it weren't for the crowd. A throat clearing behind him has us breaking apart, breathing heavily, and I sheepishly meet the eyes of my brother, who is standing in the box with half the team. If it wasn't for the fact we both inherited Mom's auburn hair, no one would ever know we were siblings. While the color might be the same, his hair is short and curly, while mine is long and wavy. To top it off, Tom got Mom's blue eyes, while I got Dad's honey brown. Everyone says that besides the eye color, I look just like Mom did when she was my age.

"Putting on a show?" He raises his eyebrow at me, but I don't miss the way the corner of his mouth tilts up. Even though Tom is the assistant coach, he was Carter's friend first.

"Fuck off, Tom." Carter winks at him before separating from me, leaving me to try to uselessly smooth out my Ivy Glen Thorns burgundy jersey.

Tom only rolls his eyes. "Big man now, huh?"

Carter laughs, playfully pushing him in the shoulder. They've been buddies since Carter made the hockey team freshman year, when Tom was a senior.

"Meet you after we get cleaned up?" I ask, and Carter nods.

"See you soon, Angel." My stomach flips in anticipation. Angel. The nickname he came up with after he saw me for the first time. We were in first grade. Mom always made a big deal about looking nice for the first day of school, so she sent me in a white dress, which was ruined by the end of the day. Carter, however, claims that when he saw me that day, he was convinced that I was an angel sent down to help him on his first day. Somehow, I didn't look nervous at all, while he wanted to go home until the moment he saw me.

Making my way back to Abbie and Gwen, they give me knowing looks as I approach. Now that the players have left the ice, most of the crowd is dispersing, leaving us in our aisle by ourselves.

"Shit, Soph, that was hot." Gwen practically swoons.

"Does this mean that you're finally ready to forget that whole 'waiting until graduation' bullshit? You looked about ready to get naked right then and there." Abbie elbows me.

Taking a deep breath, I nod. "Yeah. I don't want to wait anymore. I don't even know why I came up with that rule to begin with."

The girls insist on accompanying me back to the locker room, all in the name of making sure I'm "ready."

As we walk, Abbie and Gwen are caught up in conversation when an unfamiliar voice captures my attention.

"... Carter Williams. Really promising." There's a man walking ahead of us, clad in a suit and talking on the phone. He's got a leather briefcase slung over his shoulder, and a quick peek shows me the insignia for Notre Dame on the front.

Is that...a scout?

I try to focus on his conversation without looking like I'm eavesdropping, which I totally am. "Kid's got some serious talent. With the right coaching, he'll be unstoppable." A pause has my heart racing in my ears. "Yeah, I'll be reaching out to confirm." With that, the man hangs up and leaves the rec center.

Carter has scouts from Notre Dame looking at him? That's...huge. Amazing. We've applied to a few different colleges together, but we never talked about Notre Dame. I've gotten the majority of my admissions results back, but haven't opened them because we wanted to find out together, but weirdly enough, he hasn't gotten back *any* admissions letters.

He's convinced it's because even though his grades are good, he's not a straight-A student. But, as I told him, no news is good news. I'll have to tell him what I overheard later. He'll be stoked.

I had been so focused on what the scout had said, I didn't even realize we'd made it back to the locker room until Abbie starts waving in my face, "Hello! Earth to Soph! We have to make sure you're presentable!"

Before I know it, I'm in the shower washing my hair while Abbie and Gwen start throwing advice my way.

"If you're sucking his dick, hollow out your cheeks!" Abbie shouts over the spray of water.

"How the fuck do you know I haven't sucked his dick already?" I shoot back, scrubbing my scalp.

"Because every time you go further than kissing, you call me with a damned play-by-play."

Fair point.

"Like remember that one time you jerked him off through his sweatpants and you asked me if it was normal if —"

"Okay, okay! I get it!" I shout over her, and Gwen laughs in the background.

"Make sure he at least goes down on you before you actually fuck." Gwen shouts, and I'm glad that the rest of my team showered and dressed while I was catching the rest of Carter's game. "It'll burn if you're not wet enough."

"Got it." Resisting the urge to roll my eyes, I rinse my body and shut off the water before wrapping a towel around myself. Despite my attitude, I'm thankful to have Gwen and Abbie here to give me some pointers.

My plan is simple. Mom and Dad are out of town on a long-planned anniversary trip, and I have the house all to myself. They don't get back until tomorrow night, so after the party we're about to go to, I'll bring him back to my place and we can fuck our brains out until it's second nature and I don't need any tips from Abby or Gwen anymore.

Dressing quickly in a tank top, my favorite off the shoulder sweater, and some jeans, I'm perfectly outfitted for an April night in Massachusetts. I unwrap one of the blow dryers that the rec center provides and get to work on my hair while Abbie does my makeup. I usually stick to just some mascara and lip gloss, but Abbie has a magic touch, and whatever she does with my eyeshadow makes my honey-brown eyes pop.

We're out in record time, and I come face to face with Carter the moment I step out of the locker room. He's talking with Jake, the teammate who helped him with that game-winning play. Jake's brown hair is still wet from the shower, and he runs a hand through it, pushing it back. "Hey Soph!" He greets me warmly.

"We'll meet you outside," Gwen says knowingly, waggling her eyebrows at me. They both greet Carter as they walk past, and he murmurs his greetings, but his eyes stay on me. Jake follows the girls out, leaving Carter and me alone. He's as yummy as ever in faded jeans, and a gray t-shirt that's tight enough to show off the muscles that he's spent the last four years honing into perfection.

Biting my lip as he pulls me to him, one of his hands grabs my ass as I lift myself on my toes to kiss him again. Pulling back, his darkened eyes meet mine as a heaviness charges the air. I'm sure he can sense that there's something different about me tonight.

Wordlessly, he throws his arm around my shoulder as we head out to the parking lot.

We approach Jake, Tom, Abby, and Gwen, who have taken up residence outside of Carter's Mustang.

"What do we say? Burgers at Sal's and then off to the lake for the celebration?" Gwen looks around to everyone, seeking nods of confirmation.

"I can't believe we have two game-winning shot takers in our midst tonight." Abbie grins at me.

A squeal of surprise leaves me as Carter whisks me into the air. "What? You won the game?"

Laughing, I grasp his shoulders, "I told you I did, you caveman! Put me down!"

He holds me to his chest as he looks into my eyes. "You never told me *you* won the whole-ass game!" He gently lowers me back to the ground, releasing me. "You're amazing, Soph." My chest tightens at the awe in his voice.

Tom's voice calls across the lot, "You made a game-winning shot?" His eyes shine with affection as he reaches me, sweeping me into a hug. "I'm so proud of you, Sophie!"

"Thanks Tom." I hug him back, wishing Mom and Dad could have been here before I break away, taking a step back. "Are you coming out for celebrations?"

"Both teams I was rooting for today won their championships," He grins at me and grasps Carter and Jake by the shoulders, "I wouldn't miss it."

With that, everyone disperses to their cars and I slide into the passenger seat of Carter's Mustang, the supple leather smooth to touch.

My heart races as his hand covers mine, and if I had any doubts about having sex tonight, they would have all disappeared at the gentleness of his touch. He's been ready for a while, but has never been pushy. He's the only one for me, and tonight, I'll show him.

Chapter Two

SOPHIE

The car radio's volume is low as we cruise down Ivy Glen's Main Street. Staring out the window, I'm trying to figure out how to tell Carter what I overheard the scout say. I want to talk to him before we get to dinner, without extra ears around, but I feel like this information is too important to tell him while he's distracted by driving. When we pass by my parent's florist shop, I'm struck with an idea.

"Cart, can you make the next right and turn into the lot really quick?" His brows raise up when he realizes where I'm telling him to go, but he turns on his indicator to drive into the parking lot. "Sophie Hartwell, are you propositioning me?" A teasing grin graces his beautiful face.

If only he knew.

"Not at this point in time." I wink, and he chuckles as he pulls up in front of Ivy Glen's abandoned theater, which is situated in the lot behind my parent's shop. The owner died twenty years ago, and didn't have any family to leave it to. Nobody wanted to take it over, so it eventually fell into disrepair and the parking lot became a common hook up spot. "I just want to talk to you about something."

"Oh?" His voice lilts in curiosity, "Is everything okay?"

"Yeah...I mean..." A small laugh of disbelief escapes me. "Did you know a scout was going to be at the game tonight?"

Carter's mouth gapes open. His surprise is understandable. Ivy Glen is such a small town, there wouldn't be a scout at a game unless they were looking at someone specific. "What? Tell me what happened." He puts the car in park and shifts, angling his body towards me, waiting for me to speak.

"I was leaving the game earlier, and there was this scout from Notre Dame talking about you on the phone...." excitement seizes me. "I think they're going to try to get you in."

His face goes slack for a moment, and he shakes his head. "I don't think so, Soph. My grades barely meet the minimum requirements. I haven't even heard back from any of our applied schools yet. I don't think I would cut it for Notre Dame, even *if* they wanted me."

"I know what I heard." My voice is more aggressive than I mean for it to be, but why isn't he listening to me? "The guy said you have some 'serious talent' and that with the right coaching, you'd be 'unstoppable.'"

He's fighting his smile, but it breaks through anyway. "That's what he said?" Hope lines his voice.

I nod, and before I know what's happening, Carter is kissing me, his hands on my face as he holds me to him. Kissing him back just as fiercely, heat curls in my belly and my thighs clench together. His tongue dips into my mouth and a moan escapes me at the contact. God, that is *good*.

Wait. This is *not* what I came here to do, no matter how good it is.

Forcing myself back, I shake my head, smiling. "And you accuse *me* of propositioning *you*." Meeting his eyes, I try to make my tone as authoritative as possible. "You should talk to your parents. Maybe they've been trying to contact them."

A muscle in his jaw ticks, but he nods, putting his hands

back on the wheel. "I will." I know his parents are a sore spot for him sometimes. His dad, specifically. He's not the warmest man around, to put it lightly.

Carter's dad is super strict, which makes it hard for him to feel like he has Dad's approval.

Unexpectedly, Carter drops his hands from the wheel, kissing me again. This time, though, it's fast and slightly possessive

"I love you." He breathes.

"I love you too."

He looks over my face for a moment longer, as if searching for something. He must find it, because he gives a small nod before turning back towards the steering wheel and putting the car back in drive..

My phone beeps, and I pull it out to a text message from Abbie.

> Abbie: Don't tell me you stopped to get the
> 8==D

Stifling a laugh, I type out a quick reply.

> Me: Down, girl. We're coming. I just had to talk to him about something.

> Abbie: Oh, is that what the kids are calling it these days? ;)

> Me: Can you order us a couple of cokes and double cheeseburgers?

> Abbie: You're lucky I love you.

"That, Gwen?" Carter asks, pulling out of the parking lot and resuming our journey to Sal's.

"Abbie," I inform him, tucking my phone back in my pocket, "You know how she gets when she's hungry."

"Yeah, almost as hangry as you," he teases, and I swat his arm.

We pull into the parking lot of Sal's, the best burger joint in Ivy Glen. The bell jingles as we open the door, and we're greeted by Sal himself, nodding to us from behind the diner-style bar. "Your buddies are in the back." Sal is probably 70 by now, but he still works six days a week, always looking sharp as a tack in his crisp white shirt, white and red striped apron, and paper hat.

We used to think that he had no choice but to work so many days, but when the hockey team did a fundraiser for him to help him retire, he just laughed and told us he would go crazy if he was home all day and that the diner is his life.

"Thanks Sal!" I call and blow him a kiss, causing Sal to chuckle and shake his head. Carter takes my hand, twining our fingers together, as we make our way to the back of the diner.

Almost all the booths are full, both mine and Carter's teammates taking up half of them. There's a round of wolf-whistles and cheers when his teammates spot us, calling out to the man of the hour. I don't mind the spotlight necessarily, but I don't go out of my way to be in the center of it. After I started dating Carter, I learned hard and fast that many people who were trying to be my friend were anything but genuine, especially a lot of the girls. That's why I prefer to stick with a close group of friends who I know I can trust. Regardless, when you're dating the golden boy who's always on the town's radar, you're bound to get noticed. Luckily our friends got here ahead of us, and we have two spots saved for us by Abbie, Gwen, Tom and Jake.

Even though Tom is a couple of years older than us, the two of us have always been close, and since our house used to be the primary hang out spot, our friend groups would inevitably come together. After Tom graduated high school, most of his friends moved away from the small town life, while Tom stayed behind and fell in love. When he accepted the job of assistant coach, he was worried our friends wouldn't want to see him outside of practice or games, that it might be too weird.

But I believe Carter's exact words were "Cut that shit out, Tom, you're stuck with us."

"Took you long enough!" Abbie dramatically sighs, just as a waitress brings our food out.

"Thanks for ordering, Angel." Carter's mouth is so close to my ear I can feel his breath, and dammit, I do not want to be horny at the same table as my brother.

My cheeks must be red, because Abby and Gwen are both stifling laughs as they stuff their faces full of fries.

Carter only chuckles, shaking his head. "Your friends are weird."

"Hey!" Abbie says, her green eyes twinkling as she swallows a mouth full of fries. "We're *your* friends too."

"She's right, you know," Gwen adds, her blonde curls swaying as she stirs her milkshake. "You spend too much time with us not to be."

"Fair enough," Carter laughs, looking pointedly at Abbie and Gwen. "Then let me amend my statement: our friends are weird."

Abbie gives a satisfied nod. "Damn straight."

Tom sighs. "All you guys are weird."

Jake elbows him. "Says the assistant coach hanging out with a bunch of high schoolers."

Tom reddens, "Hey, as of..." He checks the time on his phone, "Thirty minutes ago, I am not acting as assistant coach. I'm just having a celebratory dinner with my sister, best friend, and their friends."

"Don't let Sarah hear you call him your best friend," I warn, shoving a fry into my mouth. Sarah is Tom's wife. They weren't together very long before they had a surprise pregnancy, but Tom's marriage proposal was based on nothing but love. They got married almost two years ago at the age of nineteen, and have since had an adorable one-year-old son, Jordan, who has me as his favorite auntie.

Tom rolls his eyes, "Wife-best friend and friend-best friend are different."

"What about your son?" Jake asks, ever the pot stirrer, "You mean to tell me you'd pick this wingnut," he tosses a fry at Carter, "over your sickeningly adorable spawn?"

"*I'm* Jordan's best friend," I grin. "His first word was 'Fee-Fee'"

"Fee-fee's not even a word!" Tom argues. "He hasn't even said Mama or Dada yet."

"Fee-fee is *so* a word, especially when he only said it because I was trying to brainwash him into saying 'Sophie' first."

Our table dissolves into laughter, and soon we're all walking out of the diner and to our cars.

"Hey Soph?" Carter asks me, once we're driving to the party, laying his hand on mine in between gear shifts as we ride in comfortable quiet.

"Hmm?" I turn from looking out the window to face him.

"What would you do..." He clears his throat, "What if... against all odds, I went to Notre Dame?" Ah. He's thinking of the scout I told him about.

"I'd go with you, just like we talked about."

"You would?"

"Well, maybe not to Notre Dame. I mean, my grades are no joke, but I would have missed the deadline for applications by now. So have you, but I think if they really want you for the hockey team, they'll figure something out. But I would go to a local college by Notre Dame." My fingers tighten in his as he nods at my words, "Maybe I would apply for the next semester and try to join you. I can always get a part-time job or apply for student loans to make it work. I mean...It's you and me, Cart." My parents are well off enough that we could afford a small local college without much need for additional financial aid, but Notre Dame? That's way outside of our price range.

"I don't want you to have to take out loans." He looks pensive. "I would work too, to help you pay for it."

Snorting, I shake my head. "You would be too busy with hockey to do that, babe." His jaw clenches in response to my words. "Hey," I say softly, and he briefly glances at me, his face softening. "This is all hypothetical, right? You haven't even talked to your parents yet. Let's figure it out when we know if there's something to figure out. We promised we would stay together for college, and we will. I love hockey, but I don't want it as my future career like you do. As long as we do this together, it will all work out."

His eyes soften, and he nods, bringing my hand to his mouth, kissing the back of it, "It's you and me, Soph. We'll do it together, *I promise.*"

"You and me." I smile, repeating our mantra.

Finally, we pull up to the parking lot at Ivy Glen lake, and I can't wait to join the party. There's string lights from the cabins on the lakeside that connect to poles near the water, casting the area in a warm glow. There are a couple of different speakers blasting out music and crowds of people dancing and talking. The entire school must be here.

Ivy Glen Lake is the most popular party spot in town, but all the adults pretend to know nothing about it. Even though they all partied here when they were in highschool, cops never show up to bust underage drinking, and parents never object to their kids coming out here. It probably helps that the unofficial rule is whoever is hosting needs to have a car service available until 3am so everyone always gets home safe. When I told my mom about the party over the phone earlier, all she said was, "have fun, sweetie."

Carter turns off the car, and shifts in his seat to face me, causing his muscles to ripple deliciously under his shirt, "You ready?"

Am I ready? Taking in his icy blue eyes, wavy black hair, and chiseled features, I can't help but lean over to capture his lips with mine in a brief kiss. "More than you know," I whisper..

My eyes dart down to his heart-stopping smile before he playfully nips my lower lip, his eyes darkening with need. "Don't be giving me any ideas," he murmurs, threading his hand through my hair at the nape of my neck before pulling me in for a deeper kiss.

Holy ever-loving fuck.

It takes all of my self control to not order him to drive to my house right this second.

A car horn beeps, and we jump apart, scowling at Tom and Jake who just pulled in next to us, laughing at our expense.

Sighing, I unbuckle my seatbelt and move to open the door.

"Hey Williams, think you can keep your hands off my sister long enough to enjoy the party?" Tom laughs, talking to Carter while he gets out of his car.

"Yeah, yeah." Carter rolls his eyes as Abbie and Gwen come from our other side, sandwiching me between them.

"New rule." Abbie announces, "We get you most of the night, since you'll be busy later."

They both snicker as Carter looks at me questioningly.

As much as I want to celebrate our victories with our friends, I really hope this evening flies by.

Chapter Three

SOPHIE

THE MUSIC IS THUMPING THROUGH THE loudspeakers as our little group makes its way past the makeshift dance area, towards the coolers with the drinks. Abbie and Gwen break off from me, rushing to the dance floor and effectively abandoning their plan to stick to my side all night, allowing Carter to swoop in and wrap his arm around my waist.

People call out to us as we pass by. Well, mostly at Carter, and he waves to his adoring fans as he tightens his grip on me, pulling me closer to his side. Melting into him is easy, and I do just that as we walk the rest of the way to the ice chests with all the drinks.

Jake and Tom are ahead of us, rifling through the drinks, and by the time we reach them, Jake has beers, and Tom has sodas.

"To the heroes of the evening!" Jake grins at us as he tries to hand over some cold cans of beer.

Carter waves him away, rubbing his hand on the side of my arm. "Nah, man, I'm driving with precious cargo tonight." Butterflies break out in my stomach like I'm some kind of preteen with my first crush.

Tom nods approvingly, passing him a can of orange soda

instead. "Smart man. I'm only staying for a toast, then I need to get home."

Shaking my head, I pluck one of the cans from Jake's arms and pop it open. "I'm not driving." I shrug in response to Tom's scowl.

"It doesn't matter if you're not driving, you shouldn't—"

"Oh, fuck off Tom," I roll my eyes, "Don't act all high and mighty like I didn't catch you sneaking through the front door wasted 9/10 weekends back when you were in school." Not to mention the fact that I covered for him with Mom and Dad every single time he needed me to.

"Why is everyone telling me to fuck off tonight?" Tom mutters.

"Because you're acting like you came to the party as a chaperone instead of my brother." He scowls at me, and I groan in frustration. "I'll stick to one, okay? Don't get your panties in a twist." Tom seems satisfied by that answer, since he nods once to me before cracking open his own soda. I can't give him too hard of a time. I know that becoming a parent gives you perspective on a lot of things.

Jake claps a hand on Tom's shoulder, waggling his eyebrows. "Panties, huh? I always pegged you for a boxers kind of guy."

A laugh overtakes me, and I double over, almost shooting beer out of my nose, right as Abbie and Gwen come over to us. Gwen gives me a hearty pat on the back as she asks, "Why are we talking about Tom's panties?"

Tom only shakes his head, chuckling, "You guys are assholes."

"But we're *your* assholes," Jake laughs, shoving an elbow into his ribs.

Moving off to the side of the make-shift dance floor, more of Carter's teammates join us and soon the conversation shifts to play-by-plays of both games. Distracted and most likely bored of the conversation the boys are having, Abbie decides to redirect the focus as she starts jumping up and down, excitement in her voice. "Oh, Sophie! I forgot to tell you! Your parents facetimed me during your game!"

"They did?" My eyebrows shoot up.

"Yeah, it was so cute! They caught your winning goal and wanted me to tell you how proud they are of you."

My heart leaps at the fact my parents saw my winning shot. They've been to every single game I've ever played, so it was weird not having them there today. Though one good thing about them being out of town means I have the house all to myself for my plans with Carter later.

"You know they would have been there if it wasn't for that wiring issue that made them put the games off." Tom says, taking a sip of his soda.

He's right. I know he is. They would never intentionally miss a single one of my games, let alone the most important one of my life so far.

My parents planned their 25th anniversary trip six months ago, pre-paid for everything, and purposely scheduled it for *after* hockey season. How could they have known the rec center's wiring would go berserk, causing them to not have power the weekend the championships were supposed to take place?

"We're all proud of you, Angel." Carter presses a kiss to my head, causing a blush to rise up to my cheeks.

"Not as proud as I am of *you*." I poke a finger at his nose.

"We're all proud of both of you." Gwen rolls her eyes, then shoves her drink in the middle of the circle in a toast. "To Sophie and Carter!"

Tom, Jake, Abbie, and Gwen all echo her while smashing their cans together, causing laughter to erupt when half their drinks spill out onto the floor. Tilting my head up to glance at Carter, I see he's already looking at me. His icy blues shine with warmth as his eyes rove my face like he wants to memorize every inch of me.

I hope this is the look he gives me when we're both naked later.

An hour later, Tom's gone home, and everyone's dancing together to Taylor Swift's "Lavender Haze", our bodies writhing to the music. Abbie and Gwen are tipsy, laughing and grinding on Jake. His expression looks like he won the lottery.

Swaying side to side, I feel the heat of Carter's back behind me as his hands rest on my hips. Standing at six foot, he's the perfect height to my five-foot-five." My hand reaches up to drape on the back of his neck, and his head comes down next to mine as he peppers kisses on my exposed shoulder. That's it. This is officially my new favorite song.

Lost in the sensations of his hot mouth on my skin, a needy moan escapes me, and Carter moves closer, his hard length pressing right below the small of my back.

Fuck.

Teasing him, I grind my hips back, rubbing his erection through his jeans, causing him to curse into my neck. "Careful, Sophie, unless you're planning on getting me out of here and taking care of the problem you just caused."

Swiftly, I take a step forward, his hands falling from my body, and turn to face him, biting my lip.

His eyes darken as he takes in my expression.

Overcome with need, I grab his hand, quickly pulling him away from the music. Everybody is too busy dancing to notice us slip away as I lead him behind one of the cabins. During the summer, these cabins are filled with families enjoying time on the lake, but since it's early April, they provide the perfect cover for what I want to do with Carter.

"Where are we going?" His voice is rough with desire.

"Shh! I'm enacting my plan." I giggle, backing up until I've squished myself between Carter and the wall of the cabin.

"Your plan?" He raises an eyebrow at me, grabbing my other hand and putting them on either side of my head against the wall.

My stomach flips as I breathe in his scent.

"It's a two-part plan, really." My voice is breathless.

"Are you going to clue me in on this plan?" He smirks.

"I guess you'll have to find out as we go."

"I bet I can guess what the first part is," he practically purrs before slamming his lips down on mine. The kiss is electric, our tongues dancing together as the heat between us intensifies. Carter's hands slide down my arms, leaving a trail of goosebumps in their wake, before tangling in my hair, pulling me closer. I melt into him, my fingers tracing the muscles of his back through his shirt, feeling the tension there.

His hands begin to roam, finding their way under my shirt, the featherlight softness of his touch setting my skin alight. I gasp against his lips as his fingers find the bare skin of my lower back, pulling me flush against him. The wood of the cabin presses into my back, grounding me as the world fades away around us.

My hands slip under his shirt, exploring the hard planes of his chest. He groans softly, the sound vibrating through me, sparking a deeper desire. His lips leave mine, trailing hot kisses down my neck, making me arch into him, seeking more.

"Oh, Carter," I gasp, my nerve endings lighting up at his touch.

I move my hands lower, fingering the waistband of his jeans, feeling the heat of his skin. He shivers under my touch, a low growl escaping his throat as he claims my lips again, this time with a fierce intensity that leaves us both breathless.

A sigh escapes me as he reaches up under my bra and cups my breast, his thumb teasing my nipple until it hardens under his touch. His other hand grips my waist, pulling me closer until I can feel his hardness pressing against me, making my pulse race.

My hand slides down over his erection, rubbing him through his pants, and my mouth swallows the groan that rumbles out of him. He starts grinding against my hand, his breath hitching as he kisses me harder.

Withdrawing my hand, I hook my leg up around his waist. He understands what I'm requesting, and lifts me from under my thighs, pinning me between him and the wall of the cabin. His pulsing cock pushes against my center, mere layers of clothing the only thing separating us.

He continues to devour me, and my hips grind against him, seeking friction against where I want him the most. Before long, we're practically humping each other against the wall. Each time his length pushes against my core, a breathy moan escapes me.

"Shit, Sophie." Carter pulls away, his eyes glassy, breathing hard. "If you keep doing that, I'm going to come in my pants."

"Then I guess we should take this somewhere else."

"Somewhere else?"

"My house, more precisely. Part two of my plan and all that." I level him with what I hope is a seductive look. "You, me, this, but no clothes. And preferably a bed."

"What about after graduation?" His eyes search my face, looking for any hesitation or doubt. He won't find it.

"Having that rule made me feel in control...safe." I shake my head. "But I'm safe with you, Carter. I know I am. Let's head to my place," I whisper, the words tingling with excitement.

Carter grins, setting me down gently. His hand cups my cheek. "I can't believe I'm lucky enough to have you."

Holding hands, we come out from behind the cabin, nobody the wiser of our disappearance. "Ready?" Carter looks at me.

"Almost." I squeeze his hand.

After ensuring Jake will make sure Abby and Gwen get home safely, we all but run back to the mustang, and I let out a squeal as he playfully slaps my ass along the way.

We slide into his car, the doors shutting behind us, and the engine revs to life. He leans over, cupping my face, and pulls my mouth to his in a desperate kiss. Just as quickly, he pulls away, breathing heavily.

"Let's get out of here." I tell him, knowing that somehow, the rest of this night will change everything.

"Gladly," he answers, squeezing my thigh before putting the car in drive, tires squealing as we head off into the night.

THE HOUSE IS DARK WHEN I CRACK THE FRONT DOOR open, and as soon as I have it locked behind us, Carter is on me. His mouth envelops mine in a possessive kiss as he pushes me against the door, his fingers threading through the back of my hair.

A moan escapes me as his tongue plunders into my mouth, allowing me to taste him fully. His responding growl sends heat down to my pussy, which is already clenching in anticipation. He shoves a knee between my legs, allowing me to grind my pulsing clit down on his clothed leg.

As far as the world knows, Carter is the perfect gentleman. Parents love him — he's polite, kind, and charismatic. I'm the only one who gets to see this feral, unrestrained side of him. He's always held back slightly for me, knowing what my boundaries are. But now that I've made it clear that fucking is definitely on the table tonight, all bets are off.

His mouth leaves mine, trailing down my neck, as his hands grasp my waist, grinding me harder against his leg.

"Carter?" I gasp, the sensation of his lips on my skin

combined with the stimulation on my clit making me feel a bit frazzled.

"Hm?" His lips don't leave my neck as he licks and sucks, and *fuck*, is he going to leave a hickey? He's kissed my neck before, but never so intensely. It must be the thought of finally having sex making him get carried away...maybe I like the idea of him marking me like that.

"Part two of my plan requires a...um..." my mind swims as he continues his onslaught of my neck, my nerves alight at the overwhelming stimulation, "a bed." I finally get out, and he places a kiss on my jaw under my ear before kissing me on the lips again. He nods once, giving me a heart-stopping grin.

Before I know it, he's bent down, tossing me over his shoulder as if I'm no heavier than a sack of grain. A squeal of laughter escapes me as he eagerly bounds up the stairs, playfully tossing me on the bed.

Sitting up on my elbows, I watch as he prowls towards me, a glimpse of the predator he is on the ice. He crawls onto the bed, his black hair flopping into his eyes as he cages himself over me with his elbows on either side of my head.

Tipping my head up, I capture his lips with mine, slowly laying my head back on the pillow as he melts into me. His body presses into mine, and I again feel the hard length of his cock pushing against me. My hands travel to the bottom of his shirt, trying to pull it off of him. He briefly breaks the kiss to remove the shirt completely, then returns to me full force.

Fumbling with the buckle of his belt, I try to shimmy his pants off before he rolls onto his back, arching his back to take them off himself. Taking advantage of the break in activity, I peel my shirt and jeans off as fast as I can, ready when he turns back to face me.

He's laying on his side, with his head propped up on his hand. His muscles are on full display, his boxer-briefs tenting with his obvious erection. He doesn't notice me ogling him because his eyes are roving my body. They travel up my legs, lingering on the little pink thong covering me. Tingles shoot through me as he licks his lips, gazing up to the matching pink bra that does wonders for my tits, before landing on my face, his eyes softening.

He pulls me closer to him, causing me to turn on my side to face him. "You are so perfect, Sophie." It's not like he hasn't seen my body like this before. I mean, summer swims at the lake and all that. But there's something innately more intimate about this.

We kiss again, slower this time. My mouth immediately opens to him, our tongues dancing lazily together. His free hand trails down from my neck to my shoulders before he reaches behind me, unhooking my bra.

I manage to shimmy out of it without disconnecting our lips, and his hand cups my breast, his thumb brushing delicately over my nipple. A shiver shoots through me, and he kisses down my throat, over the tops of my breasts before taking my nipple completely into his mouth. My hands tangle in his hair as his hand brushes over the top of my thong, sending a jolt straight through me.

"Oh, *Carter*." My voice is breathless as he dips his fingers past my underwear, swiping through my folds. They swirl and tease over my clit at the same tempo as his tongue twirls over my nipple.

A moan escapes me as he delves two fingers into me, his thumb taking over my clit. The sensations build, sending me higher and higher until —

He withdraws his fingers and mouth from me.

"What are you —?"

"I want you to come in my mouth."

Wordlessly, I nod as he pulls off my thong, settling in between my thighs.

"So pretty," he breathes, staring at my pussy in wonder, "I've never seen it so close before."

My cheeks redden at the compliment, suddenly feeling self-conscious.

He places a gentle, slow, open-mouthed kiss on my folds, and it's easily the most intense pleasure I've ever experienced. I inhale sharply, and he rumbles in satisfaction, his tongue taking over as he slowly circles my clit. I writhe on the bed, desperate for him to make contact with that one spot. Finally, he pulls my clit into his mouth, eliciting a deep moan from me.

"Fuck, you taste so good, Soph." Carter breathes, licking, sucking, and kissing his way along that pleasure point and my hands tangle in his hair.

"Carter!" I cry out, my hands pulling him harder against me as he continues pleasuring me with his mouth. It's not long before I'm shaking in his grasp, coming undone as an intense, unrefined, mind-melting orgasm wrecks through me.

He places gentle licks and kisses on me as I ride through the orgasm. He only lifts his head when I've dropped my hands from his hair, breathing hard as I stare at the ceiling, pure bliss radiating through me.

He sits up, his mouth glistening with my release. Scrambling to my knees, I meet him in a kiss, palming his erection through his briefs. He groans as I stroke him through the fabric, pushing him back down on the bed.

Moving to pull off his briefs, my eyes go wide when I take in the sheer size of him. I've felt him in my hand before, but it was always under clothes, never out in the open like this. For the first time, I actually wonder how he'll *fit*.

Swallowing, I wrap my hand around him and start pumping his shaft.

"God, yes Soph." He pants, his head thrown back and his chest heaving with each time I stroke him. "Just like that." For a moment, I simply move my hand up and down, reveling in his little moans and pants.

But I want to return the favor.

His eyes are closed when I shift, hovering over him so I can flick my tongue across his tip.

"Fuck." He groans, his eyes popping open in surprise, as if he wasn't expecting me to go down on him.

They immediately fall closed again when I flatten my tongue, running it up the underside of his head. His breaths grow heavy as he fists the sheets. Gaining confidence at his reaction, I open my mouth, trying to envelop him completely. His salty taste is heady, and my tongue runs along the underside of his shaft as I struggle to keep him in my mouth.

His groans spur me on, and I follow the tip that Abbie gave me, hollowing out my cheeks and sucking hard. He gasps again, his hands tangling in my hair. I bob up and down as best as I can without gagging, and before long, he pulls me off of him; the tip leaving my mouth with a popping sound.

My brow furrows in confusion. "Don't you want...?"

"I want you now, Sophie." He pulls me up to him and kisses me desperately, turning us so I'm underneath him again. Quickly, he scrambles off the bed, his hands slightly trembling as he fishes his wallet out of his jeans, pulling out a condom. "I had a feeling," He says sheepishly before I can ask why he was so prepared.

He opens the condom, rolling it down his length. I swallow at the thought of him entering me, hoping it doesn't hurt too badly.

He climbs on top of me, positioning himself at my entrance, his eyes locking onto mine.

"If you want me to stop, just tell me."

"I won't want you to stop." My voice is barely a whisper.

He pushes forward, and I gasp at the intrusion, his thick length stretching me painfully. He stops when he hears me, breathing hard himself, "Is it too much?" I shake my head fervently.

"Just breathe," He says, his arms trembling slightly as he continues to press into me. Once he's fully seated in me, I take a few measured breaths until the burning sensation fades. I meet his eyes and nod, and he starts moving slowly, both of us letting out a low groan.

The burning sensation quickly fades, and he picks up his paces, his face burrowing into my neck. "You're amazing, Sophie," he pants, his breath hot on my skin. "So beautiful, so perfect."

A whimper leaves me and he continues thrusting, each movement leaving my body, begging for more. Wrapping my legs around his waist, he props himself on his elbows, and the new angle allows him to slip further into me, hitting a spot that makes me see stars. My nails dig into his back as he fills me over and over again, his breathing becoming more and more ragged.

The way he moves inside me feels incredible, every inch of him filling me completely, sending waves of pleasure rippling through my body. His rhythm is steady, powerful, each thrust deliberate and controlled. He hits the perfect spot every time, drawing gasps and moans from my lips that seem to spur him on even more.

I can't believe we went so long without this. How does anyone get anything done when *this* is an option? He pulls his face from my neck to kiss me hard, and I meet him with equal intensity, my hips rising to meet his. Carter's face is a mixture of reverence and pleasure, his eyes half-lidded, his lips slightly parted as he breathes heavily. Each time he moves, his muscles ripple.

The sensation builds, a delicious pressure coiling inside me. Our gazes lock, and I see the same urgency reflected in his eyes.

"I'm close," I whisper, my voice trembling with the edge of my orgasm. "I want you to come with me."

His eyes darken with lust, and he nods. His movements becoming more urgent, more desperate. "It's you and me, Soph." He murmurs.

The pleasure intensifies, and as I reach the peak, my body shudders beneath him. He lets out a guttural groan, and his movements become more erratic, his length pulsing with each wave of his orgasm.

We ride out the climax together, our bodies entwined, until we're both spent and breathless, lying tangled in each other's arms.

As we both come down from the high, we lie together, our bodies still warm and slick with sweat. Carter pulls me close, wrapping his strong arms around me, and I rest my head on his chest, listening to his heartbeat slowing down.

For a while, we just lie there, enjoying the moment. Then he breaks the silence.

"Angel," He says, sounding a bit hesitant, "Do you think..." He shakes his head, "Nevermind," he pulls his arms tighter around me.

"What is it, Cart?" I ask, craning my neck to look at him. "You know you can talk to me about anything."

"I know," He smiles at me, "It's one of the reasons why I love you." When I don't put my head back down, he sighs, "Really, Soph, it's nothing. That scout being at the game today just got in my head."

I nod, satisfied with his answer, and nestle my head back on his chest. "Whatever happens, we'll face it together."

I snuggle closer to him, and his arms tighten around me as I feel his lips press a gentle kiss to the top of my head.

We lay there, wrapped up in each other, the cool night air drifting in through the open window. The sounds of the night outside lull us into a state of contentment, and soon, our breathing slows and deepens as sleep overtakes us.

Chapter Five

CARTER

The buzzing of my phone jolts me out of my dead sleep. Sophie sighs next to me, eyes closed, her auburn hair still half pulled up and spilling over my arm in waves. She looks so beautiful while she sleeps. Her plump, lush lips are slightly parted as she breathes, and there's a pink flush to her cheeks, no doubt a result of our earlier activities.

I had waited for her to be ready. She's the only one I've ever really wanted. When I first realized I had feelings for her, I was afraid to make a move, that it might ruin our friendship. I never went past the first date with the few girls I went out with before I came to the obvious conclusion that Sophie has always been, and always will be, the girl for me. I love her, and I would do anything to make her happy, and that includes waiting as long as she needed to feel comfortable having sex. But man, had that been worth it? And to think, we still have the rest of our lives to do *that* every chance we get.

Guilt pangs in my chest at the sight of her, all innocent and angel-like. I had completely forgotten I had even applied to Notre Dame. My dad had insisted, and since I never in a million years thought I'd get in, I just...forgot. But now there's a scout, and it looks like he was there looking at me.

My phone buzzes again, and I gently pull my arm out from under Sophie, causing her to mumble something incoherent as she rolls to her side. Grinning at her for a moment, I almost forget what I'm doing until my phone buzzes a third time.

Fishing my phone out of my jeans, I check the time. Four-thirty in the morning. Shit. The texts are from my dad:

> Dad: Where are you? You better get your ass home right now.

> Dad: You should not be out partying.

> Dad: If I don't get a response from you within five minutes, there will be hell to pay.

Sighing, I quickly type out a response:

> Me: Sorry, I fell asleep at Jake's. No partying here.

It's only a minute before his answer comes through.

> Dad: Come home. NOW.

> Me: Yes, sir.

Dammit. I wonder if this has anything to do with Notre Dame. He never cares if I stay out late except if it's during hockey season, which is officially now over. Sighing, I glance at Sophie, hating the idea of her waking up alone after the amazing night we had. But my dad...it's better to just do what he wants now than fight him on it.

As quietly as I can, I get dressed, and once my shoes are on, I lean over the bed, giving Sophie a kiss on the head before I slip out the door. I shoot off a text to Sophie's phone that she'll hopefully see first thing in the morning and won't be too upset with me.

It's five am when I pull into my driveway, and I don't even make it to the door before Dad is pulling it open, tapping his foot as he waits for me to come inside. Brushing past him, I avoid his gaze and he shuts the door behind me...hard.

"Kitchen." He barks out, and like the obedient son I am, I go to the kitchen, finding Mom sitting at the table in her robe, sipping on some coffee. I shouldn't be surprised he's woken Mom up for whatever this is. She always takes his side, he makes sure of it. And he likes to have backup.

"What's that?" I stop dead in my tracks, eyeing the large, thick envelope on the table.

"That," Dad says, clasping his hand on my shoulder as he comes up next to me, "is your future, son."

Picking up the envelope, I note that it's already been opened, though that's no surprise. It's the name on the envelope that gets me, though. "Notre Dame?" My voice comes out higher than I'd like, and my dad's smile might have even made me feel accomplished if I didn't know what his dreams for me are.

"I wanted to wait until after the championships to tell you," Dad says, "but you've been accepted to Notre Dame, on a scholarship, and you've been pre-drafted for the NHL!"

My heart skips a beat. The NHL? That's my dream, but — "What about Sophie?" I hear myself asking, shaking my head, and pulling my phone out of my pocket, "We have plans. I need to figure out how to get her out there with me—"

"No time." Dad says gruffly, "We're leaving today."

"Today?"

"Yes, boy, today. You have enough credits to graduate, the school will mail your diploma. The NHL will pre-draft you on the condition you get some college-level experience at Notre Dame, and leaving now will give you time to train hard before the season starts."

"I..." An icy revelation comes over me, "how long have you known about this?"

"It's been in the works for a couple of months. Now get packed."

"A couple of months? And you never thought to tell me?"

"I don't have to tell you jack shit, boy." I'm making him mad, I can tell, but he can't do this. He can't make all my decisions for me.

Almost my whole life I've gone along with what he wants for me. I used to be much more rebellious, and the first time I saw him raise a hand to my Mom, I stepped in the middle, trying to keep her safe. I quickly learned it's easier to just placate him so he doesn't reach that point. Once Dad realized I would fall in line if Mom was involved, it became easier to control me.

"What if I don't want to go?"

Mom's head ping-pongs between us, watching the conversation unfold. At my words, my mom meets my eyes, shaking her head.

"Have you lost your mind? Of course you're going!" Dad's face starts to turn red.

"This is my life," I try to keep control of my voice, "I am eighteen now, you have no right—"

"No right?!" Dad roars, snatching my phone from my hand and hurling it at the wall, causing plastic and glass shards to fall on the floor. Mom flinches at the impact, and Dad breathes hard, trying to rein in his temper. He turns back to me, his voice deathly calm. "I raised you, I fed you, I clothed you. You are living under my roof. You will do as I say, when I say it. Do you understand?"

This isn't happening. This is crazy. It's not that I don't want to go to Notre Dame, but...

"Do. You. Understand?" He steps closer to me, our noses almost touching, before I avert my eyes.

Does my dad really think he can drop this on me and I'll just go with it? I take another look at my mom and it all becomes clear. She's terrified and will be to blame if I don't comply.

"Yes."

"Yes, *what?*"

My cheeks flush in anger. "Yes, sir."

Dad steps back, seemingly satisfied for the time being, "Go help him pack," He jerks his head at Mom, "And then clean up this mess." He motions towards the shards of my destroyed phone on the floor. I head to the stairs, Mom following after me, before I stop. "Can I at least see Sophie before we leave? She won't know what happened."

"Carter, no." Mom grasps my arm as she tries to pull me towards my room.

"That girl will only hold you back, son. I don't want to even hear her name again. We are different from the Hartwells." He says their name mockingly, "They own a flower shop, and we own towns. You think I got my place on the Board of County Commissioners by settling for the first girl that threw herself at me?" Dad shakes his head, and my pulse roars in my ears. How dare he talk about Sophie like that?

"No, son," He continues, his eyes narrowing, "You'll find someone of good breeding at Notre Dame. Someone whose family can help further our influence. If you play your cards right, this deal could set you up for life. But, no matter what, that girl will not be a part of it." He turns, effectively dismissing me.

Before I can bite back, Mom gently pulls my arm again. "Come on, sweetie. Let's get you packed."

I always made sure Sophie never knew just how bad Dad could get, but now I'm wondering if she had known—would me going along with his plan like this make more sense to her?

In my room, we've just finished packing up my clothes and essentials when Mom hands me a piece of paper and a pen.

"Leave her a note," she smiles at me sadly, "I'll make sure she gets it."

I nod, despair swirling in my chest at the prospect of her finding out I've left without so much as a word goodbye. I didn't even think I would get into Notre Dame when I applied, so I didn't mention it to her. I try to explain it the best I can in the note, and hopefully she won't hate me.

It's not that I don't want to go to Notre Dame. Hell, it's actually a dream come true. But Sophie and I always said we would decide where to go together, and even though I have no doubt she would push me to take this opportunity, it feels like I'm betraying her to just leave like this. She never had a preference on where she went to college, just that she wanted to get a business degree. The only thing she ever cared about is that we decided on things together and made sure we stayed together. I promised her that, and now I'm breaking that promise.

After we load up the car in silence, Dad slides into the front seat. As I tell Mom goodbye, her arms wrap around me, her hands landing on my backpack.

"Oh, sweetie, your zipper is undone. Turn around." She fusses over me while I turn around, then at the sound of the zipper closing, I face her for what could be the last time for a while. "I love you." She chokes out, grasping my face in her hands, "Even when you're at college, you'll always be my little boy."

Her words stir something in me, and tears sting my eyes. "I love you too, Mom."

The honking of a car horn makes us jump, and Dad yells out the window, "Let's get a move on!"

She shakes her head at him, giving me a last squeeze before I join my dad in the front seat, and we take off on the drive that is sure to be the longest thirteen hours of my life.

Dad isn't much of a talker unless he's telling me what to do with my life, and since he's already gotten what he wants, the car ride will hopefully be blissfully silent.

Unfortunately, this also leaves me plenty of time to be in my own head. Notre Dame—talk about whiplash. Two days ago, I was eating burgers in the school cafeteria with Soph, and now I'm heading to one of the most prestigious colleges in the country.

A college that I'm in no way prepared for...

When I applied, I didn't think I'd even make it in, let alone get a scholarship and pre-drafted to the NHL. A sigh escapes me, causing Dad to look sharply at me. I quickly turn towards the window, making myself as small as possible.

Sophie...

I wish I had been given the chance to say goodbye. Or explain what's happening. Or even ask for her opinion on the whole thing. I know without a doubt that she would have been supportive of this if I had just had the opportunity to ask her about it.

I'll find a way to contact her once I'm there. I'll use an office phone or borrow a teammate's cell. It's not like Dad is going to be with me 24/7. Hopefully she can join me next semester if she applies now like we talked about, or maybe there's a smaller college nearby she can apply to.

The possibility of the NHL being in my future is almost too good to be true, but a future without Sophie just isn't in the cards.

Yet my plans for our future stop abruptly when Dad breaks the silence in the car.

"Carter, we need to talk..."

Chapter Six

SOPHIE

I WAKE UP TO A GLORIOUS MORNING GLOW AND A smile plastered on my face, despite the slight ache between my legs.

But when I reach for him, hoping for a morning cuddle, all I find are cold sheets. Hm. He shouldn't have had to leave yet. He said he would tell his parents he was sleeping at Jakes.

"Cart?" My voice echoes the empty room. No answer. I sit up, rubbing my eyes and looking around, already missing the warmth of him next to me.

With a heavy sigh, I roll out of bed and throw on my panties and oversized sleeping shirt. I take a peek out the window and frown, noting his car missing from the driveway. Maybe he was worried about my parents coming home early?

I snatch my phone from the nightstand and see a text from him, relief washing over me:

Carter: Hey, beautiful. Last night was amazing. My dad was freaking out about something, so I had to go. Lunch later? I'll text you by noon.

My thumbs work quickly as I reply:

Me: Sounds great. Can't wait.

I watch the screen, half expecting it to buzz immediately, but nope, it just sits there, silent.

As the minutes tick by without a peep, my post-bliss buzz cools off, and I'm left with a growing list of questions. This isn't how I thought I would wake up the morning after losing my virginity.

Stomach rumbling, I head downstairs to find something to eat. My family certainly doesn't live on the fancy side of town, like Carter's, but I've grown up in this house, and Ivy Glen is the type of small town where everyone looks out for each other. If we lived anywhere else I'm sure my parents wouldn't have been okay with me staying in the house by myself.

My phone sits on the counter while I pour some cereal, and I'm adding the milk when it finally buzzes, nearly causing me to spill everywhere. Scrambling across the counter, I grab it, only to let out a disappointed sigh. It's just my mom.

Mom: Boarding our flight to come home.
Love you! See you in 5 hours.

Me: Have a safe flight. Love you <3

Flopping onto the couch with my bowl of cereal and the remote, I flip on some mindless home improvement show. It plays in the background while I eat, giving my phone the stink eye as it sits silently on the coffee table.

My spoon scrapes the bottom of the bowl, and I down the last bit of sugary goodness that's dissolved into the milk. Wiping my mouth with the back of my hand, I stand, heading back into the kitchen. The ceramic clangs in the sink, causing me to wince at the sound. It's not like me to abuse the kitchenware because my boyfriend isn't texting me. Gently rinsing my dishes, I place them in the dishwasher.

Checking my phone for the time, I realize it's only 11. He has a whole other hour to text me. It's not that I'm worried because he isn't texting me. I mean, I *am*, but only because Carter always texts me back pretty much right away. The only time he doesn't is if he gets his phone taken away as punishment. But that hasn't happened in like two years.

Could it be that he regrets last night and is avoiding me...? No. Not a chance. I feel guilty for even *thinking* that.

Maybe Tom's heard from him. Snatching my phone from the coffee table, I shoot him a message.

> Me: Hey, have you heard from Carter today?

> Tom: Not since last night.

I knew it! He's not avoiding me. But.... Shit. What if he's not okay?

When I don't answer, another message comes through.

> Tom: Why? Are you okay?

> Me: Yeah, I'm good. Just trying to get a hold of him. He probably just forgot to charge his phone lol.

Sighing, I flop back on the couch. Maybe I'll take a nap or something, and when I wake I'll have a bunch of messages from him. Or I can lose myself in a chick flick.

By the time the credits roll, it's one..

Carter has *never* stood me up before. Even if he has to cancel, he always calls and tells me. He said he would text by noon, but now it's one. Something isn't right.

I throw on some jeans and a t-shirt, grab my keys, and head over to his place.

Driving through Carter's neighborhood, I can't help but feel intimidated, like I always do. My family and I are firmly middle class, but Carter's family is on a whole other level. To call his family rich would be an understatement. His dad is on the County Commissioners Board and owns his own car dealership, allowing his mom to stay home full time. Pulling up to Carter's house, it looks quiet, almost too quiet. It's Sunday, so his dad will be at the country club, but normally his mom would have music playing, or an exercise video on, or *something*. I knock, half-expecting him to swing the door open with some over-the-top apology.

Instead, it's his mom who answers, her expression a mix of surprise and sympathy that does nothing for my spiraling thoughts. Looking at her is like looking at an older, female version of Carter – black hair, though she has some gray streaked through, blue eyes, and the same nose.

"Hey, Mrs. Williams," I start, trying to sound casual. "Is Carter around?"

Her face falls, and I notice that her eyes are red and puffy like she's been crying, and she's still in her robe.

"Mrs. Willams," concern lines my voice, "is everything okay?"

Between the crying and Carter going MIA... something is seriously wrong.

"Sophie, sweetie come inside." She steps aside, allowing me through the front door.

"What's going on?" I swallow, my nerves getting the best of me as I walk through the foyer and family room, and into their kitchen, a place where Carter and I have spent so many after-noons doing homework together.

Mrs. Williams sighs as she sits at the table, motioning to the seat next to her. Numbly, I sit, waiting for an explanation.

"Carter's dad made him apply to Notre Dame last year. Carter didn't think he'd get in. Well...last week, his acceptance came. His dad wanted to wait to tell him until after the championship game."

"So...where is he?" My voice breaks, not fully understanding what she is saying. If he got into Notre Dame, wouldn't he tell me? We were just talking about it last night.

"He technically has enough credits to graduate," his mom says, her eyes tearing up. "Carter's dad...he wanted him to start now. I'm so sorry, Sophie. He thinks that if Carter waits, he won't decide on Notre Dame because of his...well, his ties here."

She doesn't need to put a fine point on it. "You mean me. I'm the ties?"

And by ties he means small-town girl who could supposedly derail Carter's fast track to the big leagues.

Mrs. Williams leans closer, lowering her voice even though we're alone. "He forced Carter to leave weeks before he needed to, hoping the distance would... help him forget, I guess. Or at least not do anything rash like, I don't know, follow his heart instead of a hockey scholarship."

I'm trying to process this, the idea that someone's dad would think I'm a distraction big enough to take his son across a quarter of the way across the country. Mr. Williams is not a warm man. I used to try to do everything in my power to break through his icy demeanor, but now I realize I never had a chance.

"I thought..." I can't stop the words from leaving me, even though it's the least of my worries, "I didn't think Mr. Williams...hated me so much."

"Oh, honey," Her hand grapes mine on the table, "He doesn't *hate* you. He just has...plans for Carter."

"Plans that don't include me." My voice is quiet.

Mrs. Williams pats my hand. "Carter loves you very much. You're good for him."

Nodding, I will the tears gathering in my eyes not to spill over.

She continues talking, thankfully unaware of my pending emotional breakdown, but I don't hear a word she says.

I can't believe this. Carter and I...we have plans for a future. We talked about all the options, and Notre Dame was never even on the table until last night. And now, I'm being told that he's already gone? Why didn't he just tell me outright what's going on? Why did he never tell me his dad made him apply?

I'll ask him about it when he calls...if he calls. He'll call, right?

"And there's something else," Mrs. Williams gets up, leaving the room for a moment before returning with a small, white envelope. "Carter left this for you," she says, and I feel a knot in my stomach as I take it from her. "Told me to make sure I gave it to you."

I carefully open it, the paper crackling slightly under my fingers, and pull out a letter filled with Carter's unmistakable handwriting. I begin reading, each word pulling me deeper into his world of chaos and love:

Hey Soph,

If you're reading this, it means I didn't get a chance to tell you all this in person, and for that, I'm really sorry. First up, I need you to know that I love you.

My dad made me come home last night, and dropped the bomb that not only am I admitted to Notre Dame, but I'm being pre-drafted for the NHL, which is huge. I'm really sorry I didn't straight up tell you about Notre Dame. I didn't think I'd even get in.

I also didn't think my dad would drag me

out to Indiana months before school starts, so maybe we can't trust my judgment anymore. He took my phone so I'm not "distracted", though I'm not sure what there is to focus on during a thirteen hour drive besides my phone. You know how my dad can be.

I'm going to look into local colleges for you while I'm here, and see if there's a place where they post summer jobs for both of us. He can't keep us apart Sophie, I won't let him. No matter what he says, I'm my own man and I want what I want – and I want you. Always.

Hang tight, Soph. I'll figure this out. I don't care if I have to use an office phone or borrow one of my teammates phones, I'll be in touch. I need to hear your voice.

Remember, it's you and me, Soph.

Love,

Carter

Tears finally spill onto my cheeks as I finish reading the letter. Fighting the urge to crumple it into a ball and throw it away, I breath deeply, folding it neatly into quarters.

He didn't tell me about applying to Notre Dame.

I *asked* about it, and he didn't tell me.

It's hard not to feel hurt, even when his letter spells out exactly what happened. Is not thinking he'd get into a college really a good enough excuse to not tell me he applied? Especially one that his dad is so gung-ho about him attending?

Carter has always clashed with his dad. He's been venting to me for years about how his dad expects perfection and he worries he'll never be able to give it to him. But no matter how hard Carter fights him, his dad always gets his way. I shouldn't be surprised, this is no different.

Sighing, I thank Mrs. Williams for talking to me, give her a hug, and walk back out to my car. I feel numb as I fiddle with the radio before pulling away from the curb and starting the drive back to my house.

I'm only halfway home when Lavender Haze comes on. And that's when I break.

With tears streaming down my face, I guide the car to the side of the road. Ugly, guttural sobs leave me as I type, delete, and retype angry messages to Carter, so pissed that he would leave me like this. Carter is 18, a legal adult. His dad shouldn't be able to take him away like this. Carter shouldn't have let him.

We made a promise to each other. A promise that he broke as if it meant *nothing*.

After retyping and deleting the sixth message, I throw my phone down on the seat next to me, covering my face with my hands. My life has been ripped out from under me with no warning. I've never felt so helpless in my entire life. The one person I would call in times like this is the one causing the issue.

Finally, my breathing calms, even though the hurt in my chest doesn't. Pulling out his letter again, I unfold it, reading it again and again.

He says he'll look at local colleges for me. That he'll see about summer jobs for the *both* of us. He says he won't let his dad keep us apart.

With finality, I lay the letter on the seat next to me and start driving back to my house. Carter's right. I do know what his dad is like. He does what he has to do for now, and we'll make it work.

I'll apply to Notre Dame for next semester and get a job. If I don't get accepted, I'll hit up a local college.

Do I wish I was a part of the conversation before my life was upended? Absolutely.

But I'm choosing to fight for us. I'm choosing to feel hope... because it hurts a hell of a lot less than the betrayal of finding out he not only applied for a school we never talked about, but also didn't tell me he applied. Even when he had multiple chances to.

But...we've been together for years. Have grown up together. Love each other. And if Carter is still willing to fight for us as hard as I do...we might just make it.

Carter on Sophie's story continues in Back On Ice!
Turn the page for a sneak Peek!

About Back On Ice

He promised me forever but left me with a broken heart.

Carter Williams was everything to me—my best friend, high school boyfriend, and first love.

Then he walked away.

I moved on, locking my heart away and leaving our future in the past.

Now, nine years later, he's back. Not as the boy who broke me, but as a man—irresistibly handsome, an NHL star—and he says he still wants me.

But I'm not the girl he left behind. I don't give second chances, no matter how much I still crave him.

I have to keep my heart guarded, or this time, it'll shatter beyond repair.

Chapter One

SOPHIE

"Aunt Fee, you're not going to believe what I just heard from one of my favorite hockey influencers!" Jordan calls through the rolled down window on the passenger side of my car as he throws the backdoor open and tosses his gear bag inside. He's a flurry of ten-year old energy as he crawls in after it, settling himself on the seat free of his stuff.

"What's that, bud?" I glance at him through the rearview mirror while he pulls on his seatbelt. His hair is damp from the locker room shower, his blue eyes shining with excitement that only someone his age can muster after a grueling hour-long hockey practice. He turns to meet my eyes in the mirror, and it's not for the first time I'm struck with just how much he looks like his dad—my older brother, Tom. Besides the smattering of freckles on his cheeks and his sandy brown hair, he is almost an exact replica of how I remember Tom when we were young.

Putting the car into drive, I let my foot off the brake to pull away from the curb.

"My favorite hockey player of all time is going back to his hometown, and that's Ivy Glen!"

It only takes me a few moments to register what he's saying.

There is only one NHL hockey player to ever come out of Ivy Glen, and that's Carter Williams.

My foot stomps the brake so hard we both lurch forward. I'm very thankful he didn't tell me this while going forty down the main street.

"Woah!" Jordan yelps, jarred from the sudden stop. "What happened?"

"Squirrel in the road," I say, smiling tightly at him through the mirror and trying not to let the emotion bubbling up inside me show. "Sorry bud. That's... super exciting about that hockey player coming to town." Pulling away from the curb completely this time, I drive us home.

"I know right? I'm so excited that I..." Jordan's voice fades in my mind as I process this absolute bombshell.

Carter fucking Williams.

Carter *motherfucking* Williams.

The boy who had been my everything.

Memories flash through me like lightning, quick and painful. Our grade school years. Romantic dates in high school, overlooking the lake in the back of his truck. Making plans for college together.

Taking each other's virginity.

A shiver runs through me remembering the morning after, when my life changed forever. I was stuck with waking up in an empty bed. His text, with the timestamp of around four-thirty in the morning, hadn't given me any indication that anything had been wrong.

> Carter: Hey, beautiful. Last night was amazing. My dad was freaking out about something, so I had to go. Lunch later? I'll text you by noon.

I hadn't heard from him all day and showed up at his house, looking for him. The look on his mother's face, with tears in her eyes, had my heart falling. Carter was gone, leaving only a letter for me behind, filled with promises of making things work, and how he wouldn't let his dad come between us.

It's you and me, Soph. The words, which he had said so many times to me over the years, signed off the end of his letter. That was nine years ago.

Then the asshole cheated on me.

Parking in the driveway of the townhome where I live with Tom and Jordan, I'm brought out of my daze, Jordan still rambling about Carter's player stats and how he might try to get an autograph. We head inside, and I hang my purse on the hook next to the door as Jordan drops his bag before shucking off his shoes.

"Forgetting something?" I raise a brow as he tries to bolt up the stairs. Shooting me a guilty look, he walks back toward his gear bag that he had tossed aside and hikes it back up over his shoulder.

"Sorry, Aunt Fee."

"No worries, Jordy. Thanks for picking up after yourself." I press a kiss to his hair before heading to the kitchen to start dinner. My phone buzzes in my pocket, and when I look at the screen, the word "MOM" flashes at me.

"Hey." Thankful for the distraction from thoughts of Carter, I answer, tucking the phone between my ear and shoulder as I get dinner going.

"Sophie!" Mom's voice is warm and loving in my ear. "Hi, sweetie. Listen, I need to talk to you about these floral arrangements in the front of the shop—"

"Mom!" I scold her, scowling at the pot of water I'm filling up in the sink. "What are you doing at the shop? You know working on arrangements makes your arthritis flare up."

"Oh, I'm fine," she huffs. "Besides, I'm just helping Kerry with a few things. Her eye for floral design is just impeccable." Even if I do worry about Mom working when she should be retired and letting me take care of everything, at least she couldn't be more right about Kerry.

I had been so excited when Kerry walked into the shop a year ago, fresh out of high school, and asking if we were hiring. She had brought in a binder filled with photos of different bouquets and arrangements she had made for friends and family. It was really quite cute. She had a whole pitch and presentation about why we should hire her, telling me that all her college classes are at night so she's free to work during the day. She even went as far as to say that even if Hart's Flowers wasn't the only flower shop in Ivy Glen, it would still be the best.

Hiring her had been the best thing we'd done in a long time.

Even though staying local for college wasn't what I had in mind, it was worth it to be able to help Tom take care of Jordan while he recovered from his accident. Online classes had provided so much flexibility for my schedule, allowing me to take a full load of courses while helping Tom get back on his feet.

Then, a little later, Dad asked if I had learned enough from school to help with taxes for the shop, which revealed just how much my parents had been struggling to keep the shop above water and turned into me completely changing the way they do their bookkeeping. Thank goodness I went with a business degree in accounting and financial management and not... creative writing or something. No more sticky notes left on random surfaces to keep track of expenses, or the invisible "inventory sheet" Dad kept only in his head.

Spreadsheets all the way, baby.

"I'm going to have to tell Kerry to send you home when you show up at the shop," I grumble, putting the pot on the stove. I put her on speaker, placing my phone on the counter as I tie my shoulder-length auburn hair in a messy bun at the top of my head. The kitchen gets unbearably hot while I cook.

"Oh, you wouldn't dare," Mom chides, her voice echoing through the kitchen, then quickly changes the subject. "I hear they're having another town hall meeting about the rec center."

The rec center... and the twin rinks by extension. Ivy Glen Rec Center is falling apart and there's not enough money for all the repairs it needs. The owner, Benson Scott, is an 80-year-old idealist who refuses to charge for rink time for school teams and won't raise his prices for individual skaters.

His heart is in the right place, but it's leaving room for the town council to try to get rid of the rec center to put a strip mall in its place. I can't let that happen—I refuse to. I've been at every town meeting, every vote, every conversation that involves the future of the Ivy Glen Twin Rinks and Rec Center. The center means so much to the town and to the hockey community, how can they turn their back on us? On every person like me who spent their entire childhood in that rink? Who spent years forming happy memories, and have always wanted their future kids to have the same opportunity?

"Yeah, I know, I'll be there," I say, throwing some frozen meatballs and pasta sauce into my pressure cooker.

"Good. I know how much the Rec Center means to you. Speaking of... did you know that Carter is coming back into town?" First Jordan, now Mom? Am I the only one who was left out of this apparently widespread announcement? It's not enough that he essentially ghosted me, now I don't even get the courtesy of being told he's coming to town sooner than the day before? Not that I want to speak to him—the thought of hearing his voice fills me with such a sense of dread I'd rather go swimming in a bloody ocean full of sharks. But he could have told Tom to tell me. Or asked his mom to call. Or something.

The sound of the front door shutting snaps me from my train of thought. "Looks like Jordan is telling everyone. How nice for him. I bet his mom missed him."

"What about—" Whatever she's about to say is thankfully

cut off by Tom walking into the kitchen. Mom has always loved Carter and almost took it as hard as I did when we broke up. Good thing I never told her what really happened. I'm sure whatever she's going to say, it has *something* to do with mine and Carter's past.

"Mom, Tom just walked through the door, I gotta go. Love you." I hang up as quickly as possible, hoping she doesn't get her feelings hurt, but I just *can not* do that conversation right now.

"Hey, Soph." My brother walks into the kitchen, pulling a chair out from the kitchen table and lowering himself down gingerly. His auburn hair, the one feature we share, is in desperate need of a haircut. He pushes it out of his blue eyes as he stares down at the kitchen table.

Frowning, I study him. "What did the doctor say?" Normally, Tom would have been the one to bring Jordan home from practice since he's their off-season coach, but he had an ortho appointment today. His leg's been bothering him more than usual.

"Just to start physical therapy again. Same old shit." He runs a hand over his face, looking tired. Ever since the car accident that claimed his late wife, Sarah's, life and broke Tom's leg in four different places, leaving him with chronic pain and a limp, he's been in physical therapy on and off. The doctors did all they could in the aftermath of the accident. It seemed like things were improving the first couple of years, but the pain came back with a vengeance around four years ago. Since then, he'll go to physical therapy for three to four months, he'll stop going because his leg feels better, and then his pain comes back.

It's why I moved in with him and Jordan after the accident. Between suddenly being a single dad, as well as having to regain his ability to walk, Tom had needed more than an extra pair of hands. He needed his sister.

"I was reading up on a clinical trial for muscle regeneration—"

"Not this again, Soph. It's fine. I'm fine. I don't want to go through the whole process again just to find out I'm not qualified." Unfortunately, despite the fact that he can't walk without pain, Tom's otherwise healthy physical form disqualifies him from the majority of the trials that could be helpful to him. "Did you hear Carter's coming back to town?"

Trying not to let his dismissal get under my skin, I turn to pull the bagged Caesar salad out of the fridge. "Yep, twice now," I say dryly into the cold air.

His silence on the matter unsettles me, and I turn to face him, bagged salad in hand. His face gives nothing away as I stalk over to him, raising my brow. "What do you know?"

"What do you mean?" he asks.

"I seem to be the only one who had no idea he was coming back. Jordan told me in the car, and then even Mom just told me over the phone." I wonder if he's still in contact with him. It would be surprising, considering Carter didn't even bother to show up after Tom and Sarah's accident, but maybe I'm the only one he ghosted after the fact. I mean, they *were* best friends.

You would think that having a boyfriend who was so close with your brother would be weird, but back then, it had worked strangely well for us. Tom had known Carter through me previously, but the year that Carter and Tom were on the high school team together they had cemented a friendship as teammates, and later as player and assistant coach. We weren't worried about what he would think when we started dating the year after Tom graduated and some of the best times we had were hanging out as a group with us, Tom, Carter's other close friend, Jake, and my best friends Abbie and Gwen.

"He's a superstar hockey player, of course I know about him." He sighs, leaning back in his chair and sticking his bad leg out in front of him. "His seven-year contract is up, so it would only make sense that he would come back home for a little bit."

I'm probably the only one in town who *doesn't* keep up with

Carter's hockey career, and Tom knows this. He most likely didn't say anything out of consideration for my feelings.

He saw how broken I was when everything happened. I'm resolved to never let him have that power over me again. In a town as small as Ivy Glen, crossing paths with Carter is bound to be inevitable, but if I see him again, I'll simply treat him like a stranger. He doesn't deserve any more from me after he broke my heart and left me to pick up the pieces.

Scan the QR code below to continue reading Back On Ice

About the Author

Subscribe to my newsletter to stay up to date on all things Noelle Stone!

Follow me on social media and join my Facebook group for sneak peeks into what's coming next!

AUTHOR BIO:

She's the literary architect of dashing billionaires and sassy, sweet heroines, adding heart-pounding twists and turns to every tale.

Her castle is filled with her loyal husband and the feline rockstar, Freddie Mercury Jr.

When she's not conjuring love stories, you'll catch her conquering the waves with her dragon boat crew, turning every adventure into a page-turner!